Attuning to the River of Kabbalah

Karen Kaufman Milstein, Ph.D.

Crossquarter Breeze
an imprint of the Crossquarter Publishing Group
PO Box 8756
Santa Fe, NM 87504-8756

- Promote personal sovereignty
- Foster cross-cultural understanding
- Increase environmental awareness

Attuning to the River of Kabbalah

Printed in the United States of America on recycled paper.

Library of Congress Cataloging-in-Publication Data

Milstein, Karen Kaufman.
    Attuning to the river of Kabbalah / Karen Kaufman Milstein.
        p. cm.
    Includes bibliographical references.
    ISBN 1-890109-38-X
        1.Cabala--Psychological aspects. 2. Bioenergetic
psychotherapy. I. Title.

BM526 .M55 2001
296.1'6--dc21   2001042197

Acknowledgments

There is so much to be thankful for in my life, which has inspired me, stimulated me, and made it possible for me to conceptualize and write this book. My appreciation goes to all my teachers over the years who have helped to open my eyes. My teachers of Kabbalah and of energy psychology, some of who taught me in person and others who informed me through their writings, are especially notable here. My work would not have evolved without the valuable feedback and encouragement of numerous friends, clients, and workshop participants who participated in the development of this process, and to them I offer my thanks.

Much of my inspiration, personal growth, and ability to perceive have been intimately wrapped up in my relationship with the natural world, the place that Shechinah inhabits. This is where my spirit expands and heals. My deep gratefulness goes out always to the Creator of this wonderous Earth.

On a human level, my love and thanks to my husband Phil, who has been computer maven and debugger par excellence, a very important role for me since my skills and passions lie in such different directions! My everlasting appreciation for his love and support in so many areas goes to my son Mati, who has developed into a most special friend. And a thank you to Therese Francis, who has brought this project to life in book form.

Table of Contents

Section II

Figures

1
Orienting to the River

Welcome to the start of a fascinating exploration. For over a decade, I have been intrigued with the many ways in which our health and well being are dependent on factors that are not generally recognized as relevant. These include the state of the environment, our relationship with the natural world, the ways in which we experience and create meaning in our lives, and the ways in which we relate to the Divine, God, or whatever our understanding is of the Supreme Being. I have been studying the relationships we hold with the world around us, the significance we give to the events in our lives, and our relationships with God, and have noted the impact each of these makes on us. I have explored these relationships in my own life, in my readings and studies, and in my work with my clients. My clinical and experiential findings are consistently what we might expect—the more we make room for and attend to these too often peripheral and discounted variables, the more we experience satisfaction, empowerment, strength, belonging, compassion, meaning, and an overall sense of "rightness" in our lives.

Attuning to the River of Kabbalah focuses on our relationships with God and with ourselves. It offers a process for building meaning in our lives, through increasing our alignment with Spirit, in order to increase wellness at all levels, physical, spiritual, and psychological. The perspective taken is that of *Kabbalah*, the Jewish mystical tradition. That said, this book is written to be accessible and relevant to individuals from any and all spiritual and religious backgrounds—or none at all. *Kabbalah* encompasses a large body of teachings; our focus here is on selected themes and elements, which are explained in a clear and uncluttered fashion, holding true to the essence of the teachings while not attempting to address all the nuances.

Of course, every river contains sections that flow easily and smoothly, and other that may be somewhat rougher. Most likely, parts of this *Kabbalistic* river journey will flow effortlessly, and other portions may require a little more effort and attention on your part.

You will encounter here various references to the field of energy psychology, a relatively new and cutting edge approach to therapy and personal growth. Energy psychology encompasses an evolving family of rapidly effective tools, each of which uses the body's energy system of meridians or energetic pathways, chakras or energy centers, and biofield or auric layers. This energy system, or parts of it, can be mobilized to address psychological, spiritual, and mind-body goals. Issues of improving performance and expressing creativity can also be addressed.

It is not necessary to know an energy psychology approach in order to enjoy and to learn about and make use of the material taught here. If you have knowledge in this field, you can use it to facilitate the *Kabbalistic* journey that will be introduced as a path that can bring you into greater alignment with God and with your divinely given makeup. If you haven't an energy psychology tool at your disposal, no need to despair! You can still learn from, explore and enjoy this process just as fully. You will merely select a different set of tools to enable yourself to proceed on your journey. These are the tools of intuition and intention, which make real impact and possess the ability to move energy. You will be guided clearly as to how you can utilize both these powerful sets of tools as you proceed through the ASK (Attuning Spiritually through *Kabbalah*) process.

Energy, according to psychologist Dr. Fred Gallo, resides at the most fundamental level of being. Since everything is essentially energy, this includes not only our bodies, which as matter or physical substance are "frozen" energy, but it also includes our beliefs, feelings, values, and cognitions. God is understood, within many traditions and certainly within Judaism, to be the ultimate ground of being, the Source of all that exists. Thus God is the ultimate font and essence of energy. Since as humans we are energetically created in God's image, we have within our makeup characteristics that reflect the various manifestations of God. The ASK methodology provides the link for increasing our resonance with the Divine, for bringing ourselves energetically closer to the Godly nature.

So come along for the journey of exploring how you can increase your attunement with the Divine, expand the joy that you can experience in this world, and in the process enhance your wellness. See what new doors may open for you, and how you can assist yourself to more fully live the life that is yours. You can experiment and play with this system, whatever your beliefs, and whether or not you are familiar with energy psychology.

The first section of *Attuning to the River of Kabbalah* provides you with all the background information you will need. Chapter 2 gives an introduction to *Kabbalah*. In Chapter 3 you will learn other concepts that are relevant for proceeding with this spiritual work. Some but not all of these are from the field of energy psychology. Using your preferred selection of tools, you will be well equipped to proceed with the ASK process. Chapter 4 presents the goals that may appropriately be addressed within the ASK system. Chapter 5 explains specific and relevant concepts from *Kabbalah*, including *tikkun olam*, the *Sefirot*, the Hebrew letters, and the word *shalom*.

The second section of *Attuning to the River of Kabbalah* teaches the ASK process, and most importantly, offers guidelines as to how you can beneficially integrate this into your life, both as a spiritual "diagnostic and treatment" system, and as a framework for meditation. A general overview and ASK guidelines are provided in Chapter 6. In Chapter 7, you will learn about the subtle meanings and significance of the Hebrew letters, and how to attune to them. Chapter 8 focuses on the fascinating topic of the *Sefirot*, which many students experience as the core of the *Kabbalah*. It describes how to bring oneself into alignment and balance with them. Chapter 9 addresses the word *shalom*, which literally means "peace," and discusses how to bring peace energetically into your life and into the world. *Attuning to the River of Kabbalah* concludes with Chapter 10, which deals with how to use the ASK process in an ongoing manner and describes some of the broader implications of participating in this spiritually enriching work.

Given the rich and amazing wisdom that flows through the *Kabbalah,* it should be clear that the orientation and introduction to *Kabbalah* presented here is very selective and limited. I have attempted, however, to present this material respectfully and accurately. My hope is that, if it touches your heart, mind, and soul, you will begin a process of deeper learning and will engage with this material on many levels. And your exploration will probably raise more questions than it answers!

Section I

2
Getting Your Feet Wet in the River of *Kabbalah*

I like the metaphor of a river in approaching the study of *Kabbalah*. This special and holy set of teachings has been flowing for a very long time. As we shall see, currently the flow comes readily to us if only we make our approach. At most other times historically, access to the waters has been partially blocked, and the healing waters have been available only to a select few. *Kabbalah* itself is about flow—the flow of energy from the undifferentiated light of God, refracting into many qualities and moving through levels of manifestation and realization. And this flow eventually finds physical, emotional, intellectual, and spiritual reality in all the life forms—us included—which exist on Planet Earth. And studying *Kabbalah* also provides us with tools to flow more gracefully, effectively, and joyfully through our lives.

The ASK process flowed into me one night, in the form of a dream. I had been studying *Kabbalah* intensely, and also was very involved with employing energy psychology approaches in my own life and in further exploring their integration into the healing process with my psychotherapy clients. Then one night, the proverbial dream occurred, with piece after

piece of this material presenting itself to me. I began
to play with and refine the process that had been
presented to me, and which I eventually entitled
Attuning Spiritually to *Kabbalah*. After becoming my
own first guinea pig, I began also to teach it to others.
With positive feedback, I eventually presented the
approach at an international energy psychology
conference. That workshop resulted in requests for a
manual, which eventually evolved into this book.

Kabbalah is the field and study and living of Jewish
mystical teachings. Until relatively recently, these holy
teachings were kept hidden and secret, to be revealed
only to very learned and ritually observant Jewish men
who were married and over 40 years of age. (These are
the people who were considered stable enough and
mature enough to receive *Kabbalistic* knowledge). Now
the great teachers recognize that we are in a new,
speeded-up era. According to the knowledgeable ones,
we are approaching the time of the arrival of the
Messiah, when everyone with interest should be able
to have access to this wisdom. The dams have been
removed, and this flow of knowledge is now available
to quench the spiritual thirst of all who choose to
partake. Given this context, it is apparent that we are
privileged at this time to be able to learn this
previously hidden information, that the ASK process,
along with all *Kabbalistic* study, is sacred work, and
that we should proceed with great respect and
humility.

The word *Kabbalah* comes from the Hebrew root
word *kibel*, meaning received. The hidden meanings
were orally transmitted and received by generation
after generation. Also, and perhaps most importantly,
all this information is believed to have been received

from God. The flow has always been available for at least some from each generation, and has been transmitted through the centuries and generations.

This ancient Jewish wisdom explains the eternal laws of how spiritual energy moves through the Cosmos, and also addresses how we can participate in harmony and interaction with the higher worlds. Teachings include an understanding of the evolution and structure of the universe and all that is within it, including ourselves. Spiritual truths, which like all else are in essence energetic, are believed to resonate from the Divine to all physical and psychological levels. These truths are understood both to underlie and to explain the actual physical and psychological integrity of all matter and being. All that exists is infused by Godly creative energy.

We are provided through *Kabbalah* with a perspective that encompasses multiple aspects of the One God. This includes an immanent Divine force within us and present on Earth. It also includes a God Who is separate from and above His/Her creation. The *Kabbalah* can also function as an owner's manual to the universe, explicating how and why everything works, including ourselves. It explains the route of the flow from infinite light through various filters to a world of differences and great variations. We receive a picture of the soul that reflects all that is. In addition, *Kabbalah* deals with the will to survive and the quest for life's meaning.

The path of *Kabbalah* is of interest to many, both Jews and non-Jews, for its profound teachings and revelations. For Jews the relevance may appear more obvious. Historically and traditionally, *Kabbalah* is part of *Torah*, the Jewish holy teachings, and it brings deeper, richer and fuller understandings and meanings to the *Torah*. However, much of its wisdom can stand alone, and its beautiful teachings can flow to and nourish all willing souls. Consider by way of analogy the people from many religious backgrounds and belief systems who participate in yoga and chant OM, understanding it to be a sound that attunes one to the universe. Similarly, people can benefit from *Kabbalistic* teachings, whatever their religious orientation—or lack thereof. If the "God language" does not work for you, you can restate the concepts in terms that do.

Kabbalah is about spiritual mastery that suffuses the very being of the serious student; it goes further and deeper than intellectual knowledge alone. Traditionally, it also must be accompanied by a specific and highly disciplined lifestyle. It is only through physical objects, as Dr. David Sheinkin elucidates in his book *Path of the Kabbalah*, that the gap between the spiritual and the physical, between God and humans, or between the soul and the body can be bridged. The physical world provides those necessary linkage points. Therefore, while acknowledging the value of higher insights induced by altered states, *Kabbalists* affirm that our real purpose is to master the processes of conscious and deliberate thinking, speaking, and acting, in our physical Earth world. As stated by Rabbi Laibl Wolf, our task is to "...integrate body and soul, by living fully in the 'real' world and infusing ourselves with a deep awareness of our role as cocreators of the unfinished Cosmos. Only through this endeavor can we encounter the true 'I'."

In *Physician of the Soul*, Rabbi Gelberman observes that while originally, Kabbalah was a purely devotional system focusing on the ten divine attributes of God, it then began to be applied in practical ways to improve physical, mental, emotional, and spiritual health. The approach described in this book takes such an approach, while also deeply respecting the sacredness of the teachings and of the material utilized in the ASK practice.

In my own ongoing personal studies, I've found that the more I learn and the deeper I explore, the more fully this information becomes knowledge that is truly mine. It becomes ever more integrated into my life, and continuously transforms me in ways that go far beyond the intellectual. The *Kabbalah*, including the small but crucial portion of its wisdom transmitted through ASK, provides for me one of the several major lenses through which I view the world. It provides a spiritual meaning or framework for all that I experience and see and learn, and it continues to change me—I believe for the better—in the process.

Rabbi Laibl Wolf, in *Practical Kabbalah; A Guide to Jewish Wisdom for Everyday Life,* provides a clear history of Kabbalistic teachings that reveals the deep past from which it flows. He explains that in Medieval times (13th century), Moses de Leon published the major *Kabbalistic* text, the *Zohar (Inner Light)*. A thousand years earlier, Rabbi Shimon bar Yochai had handwritten the essential teachings in ancient Israel. Going ever further into the past, there was a pre-existing oral tradition that went back yet another 1700 years. Thus there are *Kabbalistic* teachings extending back for 3500 years.

But amazingly, the journey into prehistory that explores the earliest *Kabbalah* does not end there. The ancient teachings reveal that there were *Kabbalistic* instructions much further back even than that. This wisdom served to provide structure to Jewish society, and also offered guidelines for personal spiritual discipline. In fact, oral teachings hold that this knowledge and wisdom can be traced back to Abraham, who reportedly wrote *Sefer HaYetzira (Book of Creative Formation)*, the first known *Kabbalistic* text. In fact, tradition teaches that, even many generations earlier, Noah and Adam were fully conversant with these holy teachings (R. Laibl Wolf).

3
Equipment, Concepts and Tools for Navigating the River of *Kabbalah*

On any journey, it is necessary to gather and pack up the appropriate supplies before starting the expedition. We'll likewise do that here, collecting what we need.

Energy Psychology

Since *Kabbalah* introduces us to a Divinely rooted energetic structure, it is fitting to make use of energy approaches as we work with the *Kabbalistic* system.

Working with the energy body is perhaps the newest approach in the fields of psychology and psychotherapy. It often provides the most effective means to facilitate deep and rapid healing. These energetic techniques work with the meridians or energy channels, the chakras or energy centers, and the aura or biofield that surrounds the human body. Working through the energy body, the techniques can effect all aspects of the body-mind-spirit entity. These approaches are commonly used to decrease anxieties, fears and phobias, to eliminate addictive cravings, to produce relaxation, to dissolve traumas, to improve performance, and to bring about other significant benefits. These energy approaches also are used to improve performance in various areas of life such as sports and the elimination of writer's block, and some can also be utilized to install positive affirmations regarding beliefs and behavioral patterns.

A couple of anecdotes from my practice may give you a better sense of this field.

Elizabeth, in her late 60s, came to me for help with her bulimia or binge eating. She had attended various 12-step programs, and participated in a range of therapies, successfully treating her alcoholism and drug addiction over a period of years. However, she found the bulimia remained resistant to all her efforts. Unlike the other addictions that she had overcome, eating is "not an all or nothing issue. I can't just stop eating, and I can't find a healthy balance." Using an energy approach, this patient overcame her binge eating in just five sessions, maintaining her progress over time subsequent to the completion of treatment. Interestingly, when I first met with Elizabeth, she had stated that it would probably take the intervention of God to heal her. Towards the end of treatment, she arrived for one session tapping on a designated acupressure point, and laughingly reflecting that, "This is a strange way to bring God into my life!"

Another client, a 70-year-old man, came to see me with a year-long depression following the death of a partner. My patient, James, had written and published prolifically over a period of years, and his efforts and successes had been a source of great gratification to him. However, he had stopped writing after his partner's death, and had been totally unsuccessful in mobilizing himself to restart. After our first treatment session, James left energized and motivated to begin writing. He called a week later to cancel our next appointment, stating that not only had he started writing, he was continuing to do so very productively, and in fact was no longer depressed! "I'm cured," he said, and at follow-up months later, he continued to be doing very well.

In both these cases, meridian therapies were used, which involve tapping on or holding various acupressure points while making certain affirmations. Each treatment may only take a minute or less, although it is true that numbers of very specific treatments may be needed in a given situation. Perhaps these examples will arouse your curiosity to explore the energy psychologies, if you haven't already done so. If not, as explained earlier, you can metaphorically pack your suitcase with your positive intentions and your intuition, and proceed with your journey!

Intention

Within contemporary psychology, intention is a significant concept with reference to theory, research, and clinical practice. Intention involves the focusing of attention and the mobilization of will. It is also an important and relevant *Kabbalistic* concept, expressed in Hebrew as *kavannah*, the intention to develop spiritually in such a fashion that we become microcosms of the Creator, reflecting the Godly energy. We become receptive to any information, guidance, or insights we receive through ASK. Our *kavannah* reflects that of God, and so holding an intention to model ourselves more closely on the Creator binds us more firmly to Him.

Whether you are relying on intention and intuition, or on an energy psychology technique, you will quickly see that these are not objective tools that can be mechanically utilized. Rather, they are sensitive and subtle allies, and their effectiveness by any newcomer requires practice and patience to develop a sense of trust in relying on these tools. That said, the abilities that underlie the use of these wonderful approaches are basic to our nature and abilities as humans, and we all have the potential to develop skill in using them. Those skills then can enhance our lives in countless ways.

Intuition

This basic human ability is an inner knowing and wisdom. It brings with it a sense of rightness, and you may or may not become aware of it with an awareness of something clicking into place. People often experience this inner wisdom as peace or as joy. It gets described by a multitude of names and presents itself through many guises, including a gut feeling, divine guidance, guardian angels, spirit guides, and dreams or fantasies. It is available for your enjoyment and enhancement.

Attunement

Kabbalists understand that God's original action was to project an energetic structure that contained all of His/Her attributes. This structure is depicted in the form of the Tree of Life, which will be explained shortly. The Divine structure or energetic essence is believed to be reflected in the makeup of all that exists in the physical world. *Kabbalah* does not recognize any rigid separation between these worlds, but provides understandings that bridge the gap, energetically explaining the how and the why of creation. By developing some knowledge of the Divine energies, their source, and their relationships at the highest levels, and also of the spiritual building blocks of creation, we develop an understanding of ourselves and our world. By attuning or aligning ourselves energetically with those Godly energies, we are allowing our capacities to flow at their fullest, and are attuning ourselves to our highest spiritual potential. ASK utilizes selected *Kabbalistic* understandings and practices to provide a model and system through which we can learn increasingly to resonate more fully with those higher spiritual levels flowing from the nature of God.

To have this mirroring between our creator and us is indicative of our intrinsic Godly nature. In fact, holographic imagery works well here. We each are in reality a piece of the Divine whole, and also hold within us reflections of all that is, including the Divine energies and all aspects or qualities of the physical world.

Clinically, several people have expressed to me after using ASK that it feels like they have "come home" emotionally and spiritually. Susan, a professional woman in her late 40s, talked with me regarding some ethically challenging and confusing decisions she had to make. The situation she was confronting as a management consultant was a source of significant distress to her. Fortunately Susan became able to experience the energies of the Creator flowing through her. She began to feel grounded and supported in a way that enabled her to make the necessary decisions with clarity, with confidence, and with integrity—and made it possible for her to sleep well again!

While writing this book, I was fortunate to view a video by Brian Swimme, the renowned physicist and cosmologist. It is both fascinating and heartening to learn how closely modern cutting-edge science can parallel *Kabbalistic* knowledge and understanding. Dr. Swimme talked about how our genetic coding, our DNA, is consistent with the larger coding of the universe. He also described the universe as a "multi-level energy event," elaborating that the vastness of this energy cannot be contained in one form, and so it explodes into many different forms. He articulated that we need to enter into relationship with this energy, and to awaken the energy within us. It is through relationship with the "heart of the universe and its creativity" that our passion for life builds. Dr. Swimme expressed the need on behalf of all of us and of our planet for a cosmology that celebrates this flow and this energy, and helps people to awaken. He asserts that we can make choices to proceed with this quest. Surely *Kabbalah,* and the ASK process derived from it, can help in this endeavor!

Muscle Testing

This intriguing and useful technique is derived from the field of Applied Kinesiology. It involves the testing of muscle strength using a specific muscle. The information thus provided functions as an indicator of what is going on in the nervous system, the unconscious, and in our spiritual lives, as well as in our physical bodies and in our life experiences & histories. This is done through making a relevant, carefully phrased statement prior to each test, and then noting whether the muscle tests strong, which is a positive response indicating a yes answer, or weak, which is a negative response indicating a no answer. It is possible to learn to test both others and oneself, although testing of the self is more challenging in terms of "staying honest" learning not to interfere with results and to trust them. You will inevitably be utilizing intuition and intention, which are an innate part of the process.

Muscle testing can be used for anything from checking the most beneficial dosage of a supplement to determining if someone is really ready to address a very painful psychotherapeutic issue, to noting which color sweater will do more to lift your spirits on a given day. For our purposes, the bottom line is that we can focus on *Kabbalistic* concepts that describe or relate to specified forces or energies. We can muscle-test ourselves or our clients to determine whether or not we (or they) are in alignment, attuned, resonating consistently with that divine energy.

If you do not know how to muscle-test, you can readily learn through reading, demonstration, and practice. Many energy psychology manuals and related books, some of which are listed in the Bibliography, explain the process. If, however, that learning is not practical or of interest to you, at least right now, you can still do the ASK process. Use your intuition as to whether or not there are misalignments. You will then need to harness your positive intention to come back into alignment and to make the desired spiritual connections. You can proceed through ASK as it is described below, using intuition and intention as your major tools.

Meditation, Focusing, Breathwork

All of the psychospiritual approaches make use of focused attention, purpose, and discipline. You will inevitably make use of those personal resources as you go through ASK, even if you don't use any of the above techniques in a formal sense. Receptive, reflective consciousness enhances the ability to tune into the universal spiritual energy in question, and to strengthen your alignment with the Divine. You may formally prepare yourself through one of the above approaches and continue to integrate it throughout, or you may simply allow yourself to be quiet within while in a relaxed state, and to hold the intention to tap into the universal energy.

Breathing & breath control are important in all these approaches and can be utilized simply by breathing consciously and steadily while holding the appropriate intentions. Breath is an important component of *Kabbalah* practice, because breath is equated with the life force itself. In fact, *ruach* is the Hebrew word for breath, spirit, and wind, indicating the intimate connection amongst these concepts. As the breath is released, space is created. Godly energy can then fill the lungs and the mind with the in-breath that follows. The parallel is made between Spirit filling the body/mind and God's presence filling the world.

Realignment

When muscle-testing or your intuitive knowing indicates that the individual is not resonating freely with the Divine energy under consideration, there is a blockage, deflection, or other interference, at a human energetic, psychological, or spiritual level. None of us is always attuned with all the Godly energies in question. These misalignments are not indicative of character weaknesses or personal deficits, but they are informative as to where we can beneficially do corrections or attunements. Energy psychology, using whatever approach is known to and comfortable for the healer and client or for the self, provides a means of bringing the individual back into alignment with the Godly cosmic force or forces in question. And again, your own intentions, guided by your intuition, can likewise carry you through this process.

Sometimes a person has an intuition of weakness with reference to a specific letter energy or to a particular manifestation of the Divine, or she or he muscle-tests weak in that regard. This suggests that there is currently a corresponding subtle internal weakness in the individual and/or a disconnection between the person and the higher and more refined levels of that particular energy. Means of adjusting such weaknesses or misalignments by using your intuition or your energy psychology method of choice are spelled out clearly and in detail later in this book. The power of the energetic therapy can also be greatly enhanced by various practices you or your client can utilize. These include the use of any of our expressive abilities—artistic creations, sound or music, writing, movement, visualization. It should be noted that attunements or misalignments with the various universal energies or forces may shift over time, and in some people they vary more than in others.

4
Goals—Journeying Along the River of *Kabbalah*

Some human undertakings aim to alter the world around us. People often wish, for example, to divert the flow of a body of water. They might be attempting to create hydroelectric power, to irrigate a field, to prevent flooding, or may have any one of various other goals in mind. These people are attempting to use or alter the river for their own purposes, without regard to its intrinsic nature, concerned only with its potential usefulness. Other people may just wish to enjoy and appreciate the river as it flows by, and they gratefully receive its blessings—cool, fresh water, fish, beauty, peace. This latter group of people are noting what the river has to offer, and then attuning their needs and behaviors to be "in synch" with those gifts, thus benefiting from the flow without imposing their own egos or in any way diminishing the water flow.

Our intention in working with ASK is much more consistent with the latter analogy. We aim to bring ourselves into resonance with the spiritual flow of the Creator, and to receive its freely offered gifts. Of course, we could not divert that flow even if we wished to do so, and tried with all our might. That stream cannot be altered, because the energy comes directly from God, and is an expression of the Godly nature, which is unchangeable. Similarly, the goal as we embark on the ASK journey is not to "fix" our problems. Indeed we often don't know what the best long-term outcome might be—even though we think we do. And in the same way, we have no certainty about the best path for getting there. But what we can do—and we can learn to do this very effectively—is to develop awareness, centeredness, groundedness, and, above all, attunement with Divine energy, with the essence of God-ness. ASK is a very potent tool for the self-discovery, psychological healing, and spiritual growth that we can gain from this clear focus.

The many benefits to be accrued from this resonance can be extremely valuable. When in good alignment, the individual in question has increased potential to function in an effective, coherent, and healthy manner. And this greater health can come at physical, spiritual, and psychological levels. Many of us know people who on the surface have it all— healthy, material success, a partner or family, a good career—and yet feel a deep level of dissatisfaction or discomfort. These unfortunate individuals are people who are "out of synch" with the Godly energies flowing through them and with the true nature of life. The necessary attunement can be done with reference to a range of energies or forces revealed in the *Kabbalah*. The assumption, which clinically appears valid, is that when one is spiritually attuned, psychological and physical functioning and one's sense of well-being are strongly enhanced. With optimum spiritual functioning, the energetically balanced person can more readily enter a place of *shalom*, peace and wholeness. Using somewhat different language, Rabbi Gelberman offers us an inspirational statement that also expresses the overall goal of ASK. He states, "It is the face of God extolling us to make His/Her hidden light shine in our daily relationships and experiences."

In the ASK process, there are three interrelated but separate goals, which can also be seen as steps in a process, that the seeker can cycle through as needed.

1. The first is to **develop a profile** for yourself or the person with whom you are working. This profile depicts the individual's spiritual strengths and weaknesses or position in terms of attunement, *at this point in time*. It is important to know that the picture derived is not unchanging. The profile can vary from day to day in response to life experiences including all kinds of internal and external events. It also changes in response to energies and forces of which we are totally ignorant.

This first step or goal serves to increase understanding of yourself and of the challenges that you face. With such knowledge, you know where to pay attention. You can learn where there are blockages, disconnects, or imbalances within yourself related to particular Divine and holy energies. And of course, any imbalance in the system throws the whole structure off, just as can happen in our physical bodies. If you have injured a leg and are favoring it as you move around, you may end up with a backache. So it seems also to work in the energetic realm, where a blockage or other form of dis-ease can throw off the whole system. It is important to know which energetic centers are the primary ones needing the adjustments to re-establish a balance and a healthful attunement.

I personally first truly experienced this flow when in labor with my first child. Due to some complications, labor was very painful and attenuated. I had finally reached the stage of transition, and then the contractions halted, leaving me nonetheless in extreme pain. I thought I, together with my baby, was dying. I was very frightened, and then suddenly and spontaneously shifted to another psychological or metaphysical position. At once, I experienced myself and the childbirth experience I was living through as just one more node in the whole chain of life, extending back through all the generations, and also including mothers and infants from all species. That deep understanding flowed through me, and I knew I was not alone. The fear melted away and I felt reassured and reinvigorated in a way that sustained me through the remainder of the long and difficult delivery.

2. Equipped with this information as to where you or your client is or is not optimally attuned to Godly energy, the logical next step, which is the second goal and phase of ASK, is to effect the necessary **adjustments**. Through the use of pure intention, or with the addition of energetic therapeutic techniques, you will have the ability to make whatever adjustments are required to align optimally with God/ Spirit. This is neither a difficult nor a time-consuming process. We all can readily learn it. And once someone learns the approach, it can easily be repeated as often as desired, perhaps on a regular basis, or certainly in a time of crisis, or whenever the individual intuitively feels that such realignment would be desirable. This is the second goal or stage in this spiritual growth and healing process.

3. The third related goal, if you choose to take it on, is to provide an ongoing **spiritual practice**. Making use of the ASK process on a regular basis is a meditation, and for many centuries countless individuals have been working with the same awareness and goals we are including here. They have worked with the same sacred elements that will be addressed here. The new piece that is added through ASK is the conscious focus on the various relevant *Kabbalistic* elements *while working with* an energy psychology or the energetically equivalent approach of intentionality. This practice results in both greater self-awareness and increased knowing of one's relationship to God and of the deeper meanings of being created in God's image.

I want to emphasize and repeat that the purpose of this spiritual process is to maximize alignment or attunement with God. It is not to solve any specific identified problem. Of course, to live in accordance with the Godly essence and energy means that one is living a spiritual, well-balanced, and connected life. The person who lives in such a way is by definition well oriented to exist in this world and to optimize the likelihood of flowing smoothly with the course of life. She is receiving the energy that channels to her from God, without blocking or distorting it. So, whatever problems one might have, using ASK can only give strength and increase the likelihood of a positive resolution—perhaps in a very unexpected fashion!

In thinking about the possibilities of improving health or wellness through spiritual means, we can make the analogy with the importance of good nutrition for maximizing physical health. Many of us pay attention to eating healthily, anticipating that there may be a beneficial payoff, even though there is no guarantee that it will "cure" any given problem. Good nutrition does tend to improve functioning, and in a parallel way so does bringing oneself into energetic & spiritually balanced alignment. Moreover, bringing oneself into balance internally and also with the surrounding world creates space for more joy to flow through you. And that joyfulness is part of what brings about *tikkun olam,* which you will read about momentarily.

5
Landmarks and Navigational Aids:
Relevant *Kabbalistic* Concepts

The target concepts we will use here are ones used in various *Kabbalistic* meditative systems. What we are adding to these practices is an assessment of the energetic inclination or alignment. It is possible to find out how well the individual (you or your client) is currently attuned with that construct or energy. We are also adding the ability to make any necessary adjustments in your (or your client's) attunement with those forces.

Tikkun Olam

The larger context for this work is one of *tikkun olam*, loosely translated as "repair of the world," which includes spiritual, social, and physical levels. The intention is that through bringing about more coherence amongst self, planet, and God/Spirit, and through working towards peace and justice, each person has the ability to improve the overall state of reality and of existence. In attending to these important and sacred concerns, one is working in partnership with God.

The metaphysical story that underlies the concept of *tikkun olam* is deep and beautiful. It is told that when *Ohr Ein Sof*, translated as the "Light" ("Light Without End") and defined as the eternal, infinite and unchanging God, decided to create a universe, He/She/It needed to contract that boundless Self to make room for creation. *Ein Sof* is also thought of as the light or energy that is the source of all. Some of that infinitely powerful energy was stored in holy vessels. These containers, however, were unable to withstand the intensity of the light, and so shattered. As a result, shards of holiness along with the energy they had contained were scattered throughout creation. These sparks, being the fragments that they are, both contain the potential for evil, and also carry within themselves their intrinsic holiness. They provide us with one way of understanding the place of free will. It is up to us how we lead our lives. When we live and act righteously, the scattered sparks and shards become collected, and more Godliness is drawn down to Earth. Through this process we also can receive more of the Divine flow; we make room to receive (again that root word of *Kabbalah*) from the Creator as we do His work. We actually bring God/The Light down to Earth through our actions.

Tikkun olam has to do with both repairing and making whole the world around us, in its physical, social, and individual manifestations, and also with healing ourselves through the awakening of our souls. And so engaging in the ASK process is in itself a contribution towards *tikkun olam*. Healing ourselves spiritually is an intrinsic part of doing Divine work here on Earth.

Dr. Swimme teaches a very similar message in the context of science. By awakening ourselves and working with our personal energy that is coherent with that of all of creation, we can affect the destiny of the universe. We can play a role in bringing creation more in line with its own genetic code, which is that of the Light, the Eternal Mystery, the Creator. We possess the free will to make these choices, again consistent with the teachings of *Kabbalah*.

Letters

According to the current scientific paradigm, matter, space, and time are primary. Consciousness somehow arises from matter, and thus is secondary. Here *Kabbalah*, along with most spiritual and metaphysical traditions, parts company from science. According to *Kabbalah*, consciousness, and in particular the consciousness of the Creator, is the fundamental force of reality. It is because of God's will that the universe exists. It was created through God's conscious intent and out of primary spiritual building blocks. The Hebrew letters are the first of such spiritual energies to be discussed here and included in the ASK process.

Sheinkin discusses the use of Hebrew letters as a focus for meditation. *Kabbalistic* understanding holds that Hebrew letters are not just randomly derived forms connected to sounds that allow us phonetically to represent words. They certainly do that, just like the letters in any other alphabet. More significantly, however, they carry energetic meaning and power in their shapes, their sounds, and their numerical equivalents. For our purposes here, we work with the resonance of the individual to the shape and sound of each letter. The sound of the letter can function in a mantra-like way for meditative purposes. And the

Letter Name	Pronunciation	Hebrew Letter
Aleph	(silent)	א
Bet, vet	b, v	ב
Gimel	g	ג
Dallet	d	ד
Heh	h	ה
Vav	v	ו
Zayin	z	ז
Chet	ch as in Bach	ח
Tet	t	ט
Yud	y	י
Kaf, chaf	k	כ
Lammed	l	ל
Mem	m	מ
Nuen	n	נ
Samech	s	ס
Ayin	(silent)	ע
Pe, fe	p, f	פ
Tsaddi	ts	צ
Kof	k	ק
Resh	r	ר
Sheen, seen	sh, s	ש
Tav	t	ת

Figure 1. The Hebrew letters and pronunciations.

shape contains visually coded information, thus serving as a mandala for meditative focus.

Rabbi Wolf discusses how Adam, who had an "out of this world" connection to the nature of creation, could intuit the 22 creative forces that shape the universe. He understood the separate paths these energies take in entering the world of the "here & now." He transposed the mystical pathways that he saw into 22 distinct shapes that became the Hebrew letters, each with its sound that calls forth the associated energies. So, each Hebrew letter is seen to be a window into a higher reality

Hebrew letters are believed by the *Kabbalists* to be the energetic building blocks of the universe and all that it contains, the energetic DNA of matter and form. They are the underlying spiritual "formulae" for all the phenomena in creation. It is understood that these forms/forces/energies have existed forever, in a fashion somewhat analogous to the Platonic forms (but of course with a power that those latter forms do not possess). And this energy flows to us, continuing to manifest as we see and sound the letters.

Further, it is understood that the combinations of letters that go to make up a word act as a genetic coding for the deeper meanings of that word. On a subtle esoteric level, it is through understanding the interrelationships of the letters that the essence of the actual word can best be intuited.

These 22 letters provide the basic components or "stuff" that form our energetic, spiritual, psychological and physical bodies. It is crucial that these energies be flowing well. The Hebrew Letter Chart (Figure 1) gives the transliterated name of each letter, its pronunciation, and its form as printed in Hebrew.

Sefirot

The *Sefirot*, like the letters, are eternal spiritual flows and they are principles of creation. They issue forth from the *Ein Sof*, the unmuted Light of God. They are aspects of the Godly nature, and underlie the ways in which God manifests and expresses himself in the physical realm. *Kabbalistic* understanding is that God brought about creation through the 10 *Sefirot*, which are emanations from God, and create and resonate through the various levels of physical and psychological reality.

We can think in terms of God's imprint being stamped onto and forming all that exists. Every world, system, organism, or situation, including our own personalities, is modeled upon these Divine principles or attributes. Creation manifests the evolution of these 10 sefirotic flows through levels of reality. Each *Sefira* (the singular form) has its own specific function. Each is a mode of creative power or a Godly quality or attribute that shines through the Creator's successive forms of concealment. His/Her most intense energy is hidden through various spiritual levels until its apparent manifestation in the physical realm. Most interestingly, perhaps, the *Sefirot* all exist in a holographic relationship to each other, in that each embodies the essence of all the others within its whole, although its own nature remains dominant.

The Hebrew word for world or universe is *olam*. It comes from a verb that means to conceal, and so the word world means "concealer." It is in our planet and universe that God's energy is most concealed. In this sense, the *Sefirot* can also be understood as 10 stages of the muting of His infinite light in order to bring about a finite realm in which man can exist and can come to know God. God's power, which would otherwise be too intense for us to tolerate and to survive, is "clothed" or veiled and concealed in the energies of these 10 *Sefirot*. Through this step-down system the infinitely powerful divine energy is transformed and manifested through all levels of creation, spiritual, intellectual, emotional, and physical.

All of our characteristics are derived from the *Sefirot*, because everything is molded and infused by these forces. Usually many or all of them are at play at once, but one is predominant, and so we may most strongly reflect a given *Sefira* at any particular time. Our personalities, like everything else in existence, are derived from the ongoing patterns of flow through the *Sefirot*. In *A Spiritual Guide to the Counting of the Omer*, Rabbi Simon Jacobson describes one of many systems that use these energetic centers as a focus of meditation, spiritual practice, and character development. In this system, used for personal and ethical development, a given pair of *Sefirot* becomes the object of meditation on a particular day within the religious calendar.

Each *Sefira* is reflected at the human level in a particular pulse pattern that is informative regarding the flow of energy through the body. This understanding, of course, is reminiscent of the meridian theory used in acupuncture and in the energy therapies.

Tree of Life

The 10 *Sefirot* are represented in an arrangement known as the Tree of Life (see Figure 2). This spiritual structure is understood to be reflected within all that exists, from the most abstract and spiritual, to (in our

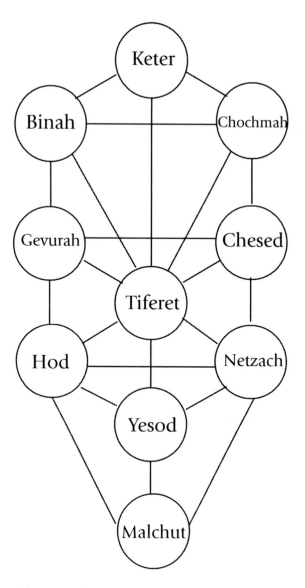

Figure 2. The Tree of Life with the ten *Sefirot*.

world) actual trees, our bodies and our personalities. Tree of Life is a literal translation of the Hebrew term *etz chaim.* Gelberman states that the Tree of Life is a spiritual map that helps to explain God's role in the universe and how we fit into the scheme of things. He describes that it is metaphorically in bloom because it is in harmony, and that it stays in balance because it illustrates the dynamics of opposing forces. Knowing where you are with reference to that tree and the various *Sefirot* of which it is composed orients you so that you can recover from what ails you, or proceed with your journey. Energy is believed to flow through this metaphysical structure in a set zigzag pattern, and it can go in both directions, from *Ein Sof* to the world, and back up from humans and the physical world to God. We exist in a feedback relationship with God, with the ability to make significant impact on all that exists.

Shalom

Sheinkin discusses the use of the word *shalom* as an additional focus of meditation (see Figure 3). This Hebrew word is tightly packed with meanings and resonance. It is used both as a greeting and a farewell phrase in conversational Hebrew, and as a wish for or reference to peace. Esoterically, it also contains the "mother sounds" of creation, those from which all

Figure 3. The word *shalom.*

other sounds emanate. There are 3 mother letters and sounds, and each represents a vital element. *Aleph* is silent and represents air, *shin* (sh) is said to have created fire, and *mem* (mmm or OM) to have created water. The latter two are both found in the word *shalom*. The *mem* is pure tone while the *shin* is white noise (analogous to white light, containing all other frequencies). These two sounds relate to states of human consciousness, and when chanted the word *shalom* functions as a mantra. Interestingly, it carries within it also the Sanskrit *OM* used in some meditations.

The root for *shalom* is the same as that for *shalem*, which means wholeness, indicating the psychological and metaphysical closeness and relationship of the two concepts. We can thus understand that *shalom* also accesses and resonates with the concept of *tikkun olam*, the repair or healing of, or bringing wholeness to, the world and to all that is within us. As described previously, *tikkun olam* literally means repair of the world, but metaphysically refers back to the scattering of shards of holiness throughout the world at the time of creation. It is our responsibility, as a self-reflective part of creation, to partner with God in the process of *tikkun olam* in order to retrieve these sparks. Then we can manifest increasing amounts of holiness in the world and in our lives. Thus it is believed that we can further creation by how we lead our lives—by the various good deeds we perform, and by our right ways of living, which metaphysically collect and reconstitute those holy fragments of light. *Kabbalah* teaches us that the details of life are important, and that we must stay involved. Actions are important for their own sake; spirituality is NOT just a matter of consciousness. Unlike in some traditions, the *Kabbalistic* understanding of the holy person is not one who lives her or his life in retreat from the everyday world. Rather, the sage or spiritual master remains in active interaction with others, dealing with daily challenges at many levels.

Section II

6
Assessing and Adjusting for Attunement—General

Caution

In working with these *Kabbalistic* concepts, we are dealing with powerful forces. Respectfully and judiciously, this calls for a specific **caution**, in addition to an overall respectful and judicious attitude.

Dr. Sheinkin explains that according to the teachers, there are two paths for drawing closer to God, at least within a Jewish, *Kabbalistic* framework. One is to emulate God, and the other is to obey God. Sheinkin draws a parallel with an adult/child situation, wherein a child also develops through the pathways of obedience and emulation. The child role-plays and copies the behaviors of adults as part of his learning and developing, thus emulating parents, teachers, and others. The child also has to listen to instructions and directions from parents and teachers even when often they don't make sense to the young mind. So it is with us as humans in relationship to the Divine. We attempt to become more like God, to emulate Her, and we also need to obey Godly commandments even when they don't make sense logically at our human level of understanding. For each of us, we need to work out our own personal balance between these two paths to God, but it is important always to note the significance of and requirement as to both emulation and obedience in our lives.

The ASK process is in this sense incomplete. It can potentially bring one closer to God through emulation, enabling one to more closely reflect and realize our Creator's energetic structure and the structure of all of creation. However, it does not address the other requirement, which is to obey. We are still faced with the responsibility of living life appropriately.

How we live in the physical world is of great importance, and our actions both with respect to fellow humans and in relationship with God are supremely relevant. Ultimately for Jews this involves following or obeying the Ten Commandments and also attending to the many other *mitzvot* or commandments that are part of Jewish practice. For all others, the obligation is to live in accordance with the Ten Commandments or the seven Noahide Laws, according to the beliefs of the individual, and his or her background and community. The Noahide Laws are understood to have been given by God for non-Jews around the world to follow, as basic ethical principles. For all humans, we find our grounding and center by a combination of emulating and obeying God. We are to strive to become more like our Creator by resonating with the Godly attributes and universal spiritual forces. We are also to live life in accordance with God's wishes as brought to us through the Commandments. And as we journey along both paths, we must remain humbly aware that ultimately God is unknowable to us as humans.

Preliminary Steps

1. Before starting the ASK process, jot down a few notes as to your sense of yourself over the past week. Include physical, mental, emotional, and spiritual perspectives. Do this again shortly after completing the ASK process, a week or so later, and periodically after that. This "checking in with" yourself may yield valuable information as to what is going on in your life at various levels. It will inform you as to progress you have made, and will sensitize you to areas where you might wish to pay special attention.

2. Before beginning the actual assessment process, enter a reflective, meditative state, using whatever method you prefer. Specifically, enter a nonjudgmental, open, focused, receptive state of mind, befitting efforts to attune with the truths of *Kabbalah*. This is a mindset in which one is curious, and welcomes whatever information becomes available. One works willingly and without defensiveness to make any necessary attunements. One puts forth the intention to do this undertaking with a respectful attitude, realizing that it is a holy undertaking.

3. If using muscle testing as a tool to obtain information regarding your energetic position or current state of being, "calibrate" or validate the responsiveness and accuracy of the test. You can do this by asking objectively verifiable questions such as what you are wearing. Making sure you get a "yes" when the muscle response is accurate and a "no" when it is incorrect gives you a more accurate tool. Ask permission of your higher self, Spirit, or God (such as, "Is it OK to proceed with this process?") prior to doing the actual ASK process. If you are not muscle testing,

use intuition as your tool of choice to determine whether or not you have permission at this time to proceed. In other words, look inward and check with your own wisdom as to whether it is OK to continue at this time.

A few people have wondered about possible risks involved in ASK. You can be reassured that as long as you participate with pure intentions and goals, there is no downside to the ASK process. It is totally safe. You will be working with the most powerful forces that exist, but doing so in a totally benign manner. This is true because you will not be attempting to manipulate those forces. Your goal is simply to learn from the energies and to model yourself upon the Divine creative principles and attributes. Therefore, you are not at risk of unleashing dangerous forces. The worst possible outcome is that you will not be aware of any changes occurring. This would, of course, not in any way prove that such shifts are not taking place at a more subtle level. In addition, changes can and do occur within time frames that we can neither predict nor control. In any case, you will be doing no harm as you engage in ASK.

Overview of the ASK Process

Once permission is received and muscle tests, if used, are found to be accurate and consistent in discriminating between positive and negative responses, you can continue to hold your positive intention and proceed with the ASK process. Each construct in turn is presented and focused upon, and the assessment (through intuition or muscle testing) is done while the person holds in mind the statement

I am aligned with God/Spirit/ Higher Power with
reference to ... energy, or

I resonate fully with God/Spirit/ Higher Power
with reference to ... energy.

Each response should be entered on a copy of the
form in Figure 4 as a + or a—according to whether the
person tests or has an intuitive sense of being strong or
weak in that particular relationship or context.

When the response is strong, there is nothing
further to be done. If the response is weak,
adjustments are made once the relevant section of the
assessment is completed.

Remember that both the nature of intuition and
the purpose of muscle testing are to tap into the
deeper, unconscious attitudes and energetic responses.
Therefore sometimes the response elicited may be very
surprising and the opposite of what one would
consciously state or anticipate. That's OK, and it is not
necessary to figure out why the response is as it is. All
that is necessary is to do the realignments where
needed.

Your energy technique of choice or your focused
intention can be used to address any alignment
problem. The treatment can be strengthened further
by the use of a variety of techniques. You (or your
client) can visualize yourself coming into a more
aligned and balanced relationship. You can draw or
sculpt or move in the form of the target letter, if one or
more requires attention. The possibilities are limitless.
After completing your correction, use intuition or do a
muscle test to make sure that the correction has taken
hold.

A Reflection on ASK

Some folks have been surprised to learn how simple this process is, especially given the great richness, complexity, and many layered nature of *Kabbalah* itself. Sometimes what is simple is admittedly the equivalent of simplistic. In other words, when something looks very easy, it may be because it is presented in a watered-down fashion which precludes it being useful, meaningful or valid. Simple can also, however, indicate a positive simplicity, revealing or working with important truths in an uncluttered fashion.

The ASK approach is one of simplicity, in that it allows whomever so chooses to grow spiritually through attunement, without necessitating years of study. Nonetheless, the progress that can be made is real and valid. We can all work on ourselves in this way without having studied and earned the deep understanding and wisdom of a *Kabbalah* scholar or great *Kabbalist*. We can do this in the same way that we can all turn on an electric light switch, without needing to be scientists or even electricians. Of course, the ease of ASK in no way diminishes or denies the great additional benefits and values of becoming more learned and incorporating *Kabbalah* more deeply into your life.

ASK Record Sheet - Results of Intuition Check or Muscle Testing

attuned   +   -

Letters

(If you are weak with reference to a letter, note if that is to its sound, shape, or both).

> aleph
> bet
> gimel
> dallet
> heh
> vav
> zayin
> chet
> tet
> yud
> kaf
> lammed
> mem
> nuen
> samech
> ayin
> pe
> tsaddi
> kof
> resh
> sheen
> tav

Figure 4. Record sheet. Continued on next page.

ASK Record Sheet - Results of Intuition Check or Muscle Testing (continued)

attuned   +   -

Sefirot

    Keter
    Chochmah
    Binah
    (Da'at)
    Chesed
    Gevurah
    Tiferet
    Netzach
    Hod
    Yesod
    Malchut

Shalom

Figure 4 Continued. Record sheet.

7
Attuning to the Letters

Remember that letters, as discussed previously, are powerful creative forces and spiritual building blocks that carry various energetic meanings and potentials. In *Kabbalistic Astrology Made Easy*, Rabbi Philip Berg teaches that knowledge of the Hebrew alphabet is said to provide practitioners with the ability to overcome planetary influences, and to reunite the physical world with the spiritual. He describes one of the powers of the letters being to act as passwords to the particular energy source of each month. ASK focuses on the resonance of the individual to both the shapes and the sounds of the letters.

Letters are the first elements with reference to which the assessment is carried out. Throughout the process, it is important to continue to hold a receptive and honoring attitude. The person gazes at a reproduction of each letter while hearing and saying aloud its name and sound, and either checks intuitively or is muscle-tested (or tests him/her self) while doing so (see Figure 1 for the Hebrew letters). Actually vocalizing the sound is important energetically. Say,

> I am well aligned with God/Spirit/Higher Power
> with reference to the letter.... or

Attuning to the River of Kabbalah

> I am attuned with the sacred energy of the
> letter....

If one checks out as strong, there is nothing further to do beyond marking down those results. If the muscle tests weak, then test separately for responses to both visual impact (shape) and sound of the letter. When the weak area is thus specified, you can do the necessary adjustment using the energy therapy approach or intentional adjustment of choice. Actually you would wait until you've tested with all the letters, and then go back and do whatever realignments are needed, one after the other. If using intention, you might hold the intention to place yourself into alignment with the letter *Bet*, for example, and hold that until you feel a gentle click or shift which is your signal that the desired correction has occurred. If you are using EFT (Emotional Freedom Technique, an energy psychology approach), you would tap on

> Even though I have some misalignment (or glitch,
> disruption, etc.) with letter *Bet*....

Then check yourself with

> I am now in good alignment with the energy
> of *Bet*.

You would go one by one through the letters where you have had to bring yourself into attunement. Then do a final check on

> I am now in good alignment with the energy of
> all the letters.

You will most likely check strong there, whether working intuitively or through muscle testing, since you have already brought yourself into attunement with each letter. If not, recheck each letter individually and continue to make any needed readjustments.

Once the individual tests clear on all letters, he or she is subtly and appropriately connected with these basic energetic building blocks of all creation. We can imagine that the person in question is then more empowered to move energetically towards and to build the life he or she ultimately wants, a life which is more connected with those spiritual essences. Of course, what that looks like is different for each soul, and thus open to mystery and the unknown. But oh what a fascinating, satisfying and worthwhile personal experiment, and one which can benefit all of creation!

8

Attuning to the *Sefirot*, and the Significance of Each

The *Sefirot*

As described earlier, first there is *Ein Sof*, the Infinite, which is complete oneness. The *Sefirot* are the creative emanations of that Divine energy or Light, which are channeled to the physical world through a step-down system of "filters," making possible all levels of reality and of being.

The sacred energy flows from God who is the Divine Source down to where that energy manifests on the physical plane. The individual is shown a diagram of the *Kabbalistic* Tree of Life. Begin this part of the process by intentionally connecting psychologically or energetically with the Tree of Life as a grounding process. Feel yourself as a tree, reaching into the heavens, rooted firmly into the earth, allowing a two-way flow of energy between the physical world and the Light. Each *Sefira*, representing a manifestation or attribute of God's nature or energy, is in turn named aloud, pointed out on the diagram, and a brief definition of it is given. It is interesting that some authors, including Myss, have noted parallels between the *Sefirot* as represented in the human body and the energy chakras.

Keter is known in English as the Crown. It is the metaphysical first center where the holy light begins its journey. The light then flows through all the other centers and into the physical world. *Keter* represents the origin and unity of the whole, the supreme will of God, and is depicted at the head or the area just above it in humans, as in the crown chakra.

As you can see in the Tree of Life diagram, *Keter* is connected to *Chochmah* and to *Binah*, which also lie in the area of the head. **Chochmah** is the source of wisdom and creative inspiration, the catalyst for thought. It is outer-directed and is known also as "spiritual will." When you realize you are on the verge of solving a difficult intellectual problem, that is *Chochmah* operating. In humans, this energetic center is located to the right of the head, and is considered a masculine energy as it stimulates or fertilizes thought, although it is itself without specific content. (All *Sefirot* on the right are understood to be masculine in nature.)

The *Sefira* of **Binah**, which is more inner-directed, relates more to content, and it is this *Sefira* which *Chochmah* is believed to catalyze. *Binah* has to do with the understanding and development of ideas, and it nurtures and gives direction to thought consciousness, the *Chochmah* aspect. It can be thought of as the womb which contains the *Chochmah* thought-seed until that thought is ready to be released into the reality of words and actions. This energetic center is found to the left of the head in the human body, and is understood to be essentially feminine in its nature, as are all of the *Sefirot* which are visualized as being on the left of the human body. Rabbi Wolf explains that *Binah* is most feminine in relationship to *Chochmah*, with both of them being masculine vis-a-vis the seven *Sefirot* of emotion, so that all stand in a relative relationship to each other.

Da'at, meaning knowing, is the combination and the balance point of *Chochmah* and *Binah*. It is also the energetic center where mind and emotion connect and an emotional climate becomes established. This is the place from which something becomes deeply known, in the sense that one joins with or becomes at one with that knowing. It is experienced and located around the area of the throat. However, this energy center is not located on your chart. It is present on some diagrams of the Tree of Life, but then *Keter* is not represented. The reason for this is that *Keter* and *Da'at* are understood to be in essence equivalent to each other, as both contain both *Chochmah* and *Binah*. They vary in terms of perspective, *Keter* still holding the Divine energy before it begins to be refracted into its differentiated aspects, and *Da'at* reintegrating the more differentiated energies of *Chochmah* and *Binah*. There is complete agreement amongst *Kabbalah* scholars that there are exactly 10 *Sefirot*, and so always only either *Keter* or *Da'at* is represented. Another way to think about this is that *Da'at* and *Keter* are never depicted simultaneously, as their relationship to each other is like that of the quantum particle and wave.

When you work through these centers energetically, you can choose to work with either *Keter* or *Da'at*, or with the two as a unit, or you can work with each individually. You can tune in intuitively or muscle test in order to make the decision as to which is the most appropriate approach for you at a given time.

Keter, Chochmah, Binah (and Da'at) are all intellectual forces or spiritual flows in the realm of thought or mind. The *Sefirot* that follow relate to emotions. The first three are internalized feelings, experienced within. They set the emotional climate, according to Rabbi Wolf, and exist in humans as abstracted qualities or tendencies or impulses. The next three are externalized into and expressed through relationships as acted out in the physical world. In sum, there are triads of *Sefirot* related to mind, to emotion, and to action. The first three relate to mind, the second three to emotion, and the third trio to action.

Chesed is the energy center that is the source for kindness and mercy. It is understood to be the most basic emotion. It produces an outward vision relating to giving and sharing, and is the quality which allows for forgiveness, be it of self, other, or life itself. Like light, it expands to fill the space that contains it, without being limited to any given direction. *Chesed* is understood to be to be located in humans at the right shoulder.

Because *Chesed* flows in all directions without discrimination, it depends on **Gevurah** to balance it and to give direction. We all know the problems caused by the "enabler" who gives unceasing support to another even when the behavior of that other is self- or other-destructive and the support makes it possible for those troublesome actions to continue. *Gevurah* provides the necessary containment, focus, restraint, and discipline, or concentration, to keep the loving kindness of *Chesed* within healthy bounds. *Gevurah* can also be understood as strength, suggesting that for one to be strong, there must be boundaries in place. We can picture *Gevurah* energy as being localized at the left shoulder in the context of the human body.

For there to be balance, the independent flows of *Chesed* and *Gevurah* must be integrated. That integration occurs within the *Sefira* of **Tiferet**, which is the center or sphere holding beauty, compassion, and harmony. It organizes the combination of *Chesed* and *Gevurah* once the *Sefirot* at the level of mind have determined the blend of those feelings. Appropriately enough, being the center of compassion, *Tiferet* is located at the heart, closest to the exact center both of the human body and of the Tree of Life.

And finally we come to those emotions that are externalized and actualized in the world through action in the context of relationships. **Netzach** is often a difficult *Sefira* to conceptualize, being translated from the Hebrew as victory, endurance, or overcoming. It is about accepting challenges. Wolf describes that this *Sefira* expresses the urge to reach into the world of the other and to make some kind of connection. Victory is what occurs as one crosses the threshold and steps into that other world, while at the same time holding one's own place, thus overcoming the barriers that separate us. In the sense of overcoming, Sheinkin explains that in order to facilitate our personal development, and to draw closer to the Light as well as to other people, we must hold back our individual egos while also holding firm within ourselves. We are to endure and be strong with a power that goes beyond that of the physical body alone. *Netzach* corresponds to the right hip and thigh of the human body.

Hod is the *Sefira* that balances *Netzach*. As the latter contains the sense of moving into another's world, *Hod* has to do with creating inner space to make room for and accept the flow of others, and with making space in relationships. It is the source of empathy, of sensitivity to the other. *Hod* is also defined as splendor, humility, or submission, representing an acceptance or a kind of dependency within which one maintains one's own integrity. *Hod* restrains *Netzach* in the world of expression, making sure that the striving to connect is appropriate and acceptable, as Wolf states, and that it matches the capacity of the receiver. *Hod* is symbolically located at the left hip and thigh.

Netzach and *Hod* find their balance point in **Yesod**, which symbolizes the bonding that can occur between two people, and relates also to the ability to focus on the other. This *Sefira* is translated as foundation, and refers to a very solid attachment or relationship. On another level, *Yesod* expresses the procreative force of God. It also functions metaphorically as the conduit through which all the *Kabbalistic* energies are channeled to the physical, actualized world. In humans, the placement of *Yesod* is at the genital area.

Malchut completes the cycle, as the Divine energy flows into the physical world where it finds its actualization before returning to God. *Malchut* literally means kingdom, and also can be translated as nobility or sovereignty, giving us as it does a glimpse, albeit veiled and concealed, of God's sovereignty in the world. *Malchut* is the revealed world, where all potential is manifested, even as the essence of the Creator remains veiled. *Malchut* is synonymous with *Shechinah*, which is the feminine aspect of God in the world. With reference to the human body, *Malchut* resides at the ground, at or below the feet

The Sefirot	Translation	Description	Location in Humans
Keter	Crown	origin and unity of all; Divine Will	above head
Chochmah*	Wisdom	creative inspiration; revelation	right of head
Binah	Understanding	development of ideas	left of head
(Da'at	Knowing		in the throat area)
Chesed*	Kindness	mercy, an outward vision	at right shoulder
Gevurah	Judgment	containment, focus, restraint	at left shoulder
Tiferet	Beauty	emotional balance, harmony	at heart center
Netzach*	Endurance	eternity, victory, reaching out	at right arm
Hod	Majesty	reverberation, empathy, splendor	at left arm
Yesod	Foundation	attachment, procreativity of God	at genital area
Malchut*	Kingdom	the Divine Body, connected with the material world; where **Shechinah*** resides; actualization	at ground under feet

*Ch is pronounced as in Bach.

Figure 5. The *Sefirot*, their English translation, and their corresponding body parts.

It is important to have all the *sefirotic* energies able to flow freely and to play out within you in your own uniqueness. They will also connect you uniquely with the Universal Source.

ASK and the *Sefirot*

While seeing its placement in the Tree of Life, and naming it aloud, consider the significance of each *Sefira* in turn and contemplate how it plays out in your own life. Notice also how you feel with reference to the qualities or attributes described. Some of them may not make sense to you on a practical level, but don't worry about that. Go with your intuition, and hold onto your intention or *kavannah* to be receptive to whatever information you receive. Remember, each of these Godly attributes are also qualities which we humans can demonstrate, at our human level and in our day-to day lives. Then you, or your client, muscle-tests or checks internally and with intention for alignment with each *Sefira* in turn.

> I am aligned with God/Spirit/Higher Power with reference to ... energy, or

> I am attuned with the sacred energy of *Sefira*....

Note on your Record Form what your response is to each *Sefira*. As with the letters, where there is a strong response indicating healthy attunement, nothing further needs to be done. Treatments of misalignments can be carried out in a relatively simple fashion, using your intentional or energy psychology treatment of choice. You would do this after testing yourself with reference to each *Sefira* and then go back and do whatever realignments are needed, one after the other. If using intention, you might hold the intention to place yourself into alignment with the *Sefira Gevurah*, for example, until you feel a gentle click or shift which is your signal that the desired correction has occurred. If you are using BSFF (Be Set Free Fast, an energy psychology approach), you would tap on

I am now releasing all the sadness and the emotional roots and deepest cause related to *Sefira Gevurah*....

and so forth through the rest of the BSFF procedure. Then check yourself with

I am now attuned with the energetic essence of....

working one by one with each of the *Sefirot* where you did not start off well attuned in order to be sure that your adjustments took hold. By the way, you can vary the wording in each of these affirmations so that they work optimally for you. Once you test strong with reference to each individual *Sefira*, do a final check on

I am attuned with the energetic essences of all the *Sefirot*.

You should check strong on that since by now you are well aligned with all the *Sefirot*. However, if for some reason it does not test strong, go back and recheck each *Sefira*, and correct and continue accordingly.

Once you experience your essential relatedness to all the *Sefirot*, either intuitively or through muscle testing, this energy can flow through you as it is supposed to. You are part of the flow of life that emanates from God/Spirit and continues through all of creation. You are a microcosm of the Divine macrocosm.

9
Attuning to the Concept of *Shalom*, and Bringing Peace into Your Life.

It is important to ascertain that nothing is going on in you or your client at an unconscious or energetic level that may interfere with the process of peace. For our purposes, peace means all that we think about when we say the word in English, and more. As *shalom* implies moving towards *tikkun olam*—repairing the world—we use "peace" to refer to the healing needed to correct the metaphysical fracturing of the holy vessels of light that occurred at the time of creation. This can only be accomplished by humans working along with God. *Tikkun olam* implies bringing ourselves and the world around us into resonance with God's nature; we must form a partnership to do so. Thus there is even more spiritual power in moving toward peace, both inwardly and in the world at large, than is apparent when we think of the word in its everyday English sense. In addition, as described earlier, *shalom* contains within it basic sounds that further align us with universal energies.

Having peace in our lives at all possible levels obviously is desirable for countless reasons. On a spiritual level, it brings about more wholeness in ourselves and in the universe. The final step in the ASK assessment process is to check out attunement to the concept of *shalom*/peace.

> I am in good alignment with all the richness of
> *shalom*, and allow *shalom* into my life.

If the response is not strong, make the necessary energetic corrections, through an energy psychology approach or via your focused intention, your *kavannah*. In addition, the individual can make a commitment towards and actually carry out some action(s) in the physical world which bring us all closer to the healing of peace, and to *tikkun olam*. Then one more time, through intuition or muscle testing, check yourself on

> I am in good alignment with all the richness of
> *shalom*, and allow *shalom* into my life.

And the final step is to check yourself on

> I am attuned to all the Kabbalistic concepts I
> have worked with today.

If that does not test strong, go back and check for weakness in any letter, in any *Sefira*, or in the concept of *Shalom*, and correct and retest accordingly.

Temporal Tapping Technique

While focusing on strengthening alignment with any letter, word or concept, both visually and audibly, you—or your client—should first use your intention or whatever energetic technique you prefer to eliminate any blockage or interference, as already described. Once you have removed any negative interference, you can use the Temporal Tapping Technique (TTT) to specifically "install" the corrective positive statement and state of attunement. For example, if you are attuning with reference to *Sefira Hod*, once the correction is completed and the muscle test indicates a strong response, you could then install,

> I am strongly connected (or attuned, aligned) with *Sefira Hod*.

The TTT involves gently tapping on your scalp starting just forward of the ear canal, and continuing up and around the outside edge of both ears until you reach the back center of the ears, just opposite where you started. You should tap with all the fingertips including the thumb bunched together as one tool, tapping with the right hand around the right ear and with the left around the left ear. Repeat this process three times, while focusing on the word or concept and stating,

> I am aligning myself with....

You can also state the more general

> I am attuned with all the *Kabbalistic* energies addressed today

to deeply install and consolidate the overall positive alignment through the use of the TTT.

Since you are not attempting to eliminate a problem but to increase your sense of connection and alignment with God and the Divine principles and energies as they play out on Earth, you quite likely will not notice anything right away. Rather, most likely, you will notice that you are feeling more attuned, more grounded, less alone, more loving, effective, and so forth over time. I recommend that you keep notes for yourself on any changes you notice, to keep yourself more conscious about the whole process. It's fun, interesting, and affirming to note and track your own evolution. This may occur on physical, spiritual, emotional, interpersonal or intellectual levels.

There are additional ways by which you can support the process of coming into attunement. It's often fun as well as useful to incorporate any artistic and creative forms with which you are familiar or with which you want to experiment. For example, people have formed postures or other kinds of movements including dances to express the shape of a letter. Others sculpt or do calligraphy. Similarly, you might write about or paint the personal significance for you of a particular *Sefira*. Some people have visually or kinesthetically or verbally created a piece that represents a goal they hold. And we've already discussed how sounds can hold meaning and significance, so singing, chanting, drumming, playing a piece of music, or otherwise making a sound that feels right for that energy might be another appropriate intervention.

10
And the River Keeps Flowing

Using ASK as a Spiritual Practice

As the relationship and parallels (attenuated as they are) between Creator and created (ourselves) become more clear, the sense of connection and dialogue deepen. More awareness and attunement to a deeper sense of self, of strength, and of joy often develop. Awareness of spiritual connectedness increases, and you can better cope with the vagaries of life.

Recall that the root of the word *Kabbalah* comes from the verb that means to receive. An important part of using ASK as an ongoing spiritual practice is to continue to be receptive to any insights that come your way. Once you have brought yourself into a state where you more fully reflect the Creator, you have opened a faucet that allows a flow of insights and wisdom and greater intuition. You have ASKed and so you receive—perhaps what you were looking for, and perhaps something that at the time you don't fully understand or appreciate. In any case, it is Divinely given, and the assumption is made that whatever the knowledge or insight, it is exactly what you currently need. Your responsibility then is to attend to this information, to honor it, and to use it wisely in accordance with its own nature and with Godly teachings.

You can go through the attunement process from time to time to strengthen and correct any misalignments. In addition, by holding the intention to use ASK as a spiritual process and using it more regularly, it becomes not just a corrective tool, but a spiritual practice in its own right. Traditionally, the Hebrew letters, the word *shalom*, and the *Sefirot* have all been used as focal points for meditation. You can, if you wish, further heighten the power of intention and the sense of spirituality by first lighting a candle, by verbalizing your intention, by offering a prayer, by taking extra time to focus and calm your breath, or whatever works for you. And you can certainly feel free to experiment and to integrate ASK into any context that is effective and meaningful for you.

The Landscape of the River

As has been discussed, *Kabbalah* is ultimately about how we live in the world. As intriguing, inspiring, and meaningful as practices like ASK can be, the ultimate bottom line is how we all live in the world. It's about how we encourage ourselves to grow, how we get on with the people around us, and what is the nature of our relationship with Spirit, God, the Great Mystery. ASK can be important for how it can enrich each of these values and goals.

Each of us has our own way of bringing peace into the world, of aligning with *shalom*. It might involve taking a step to improve a troubling relationship, or it may be a donation to a charity. Perhaps planting a tree seems right, or adopting an animal from a shelter. Other possibilities might include writing a letter to support a righteous political position or organization, tutoring a student in basic literacy skills, or whatever seems true for you. The possibilities are infinite, as long as the actions are taken with positive intention, an intelligent purpose in mind, and a full heart

Enjoy, experiment, and benefit! There is no right or wrong way to do this. Many people feel a metaphoric "click" when finding or developing a system that works for them. And they often observe meaningful and perhaps profound changes in the quality of their lives. I'd love to hear how this works for you, what your experiences with using ASK and beginning to explore the *Kabbalah* have been like and have meant for you. Please feel free to email me at MidbarNM@aol.com. I would appreciate any feedback.

Appendices

Appendix A
ASK Crib Sheet

1. Getting Started

Once concepts from *Kabbalah* are introduced, muscle test or use your intuition to check that

> It is OK for me to do this attunement process
> with these *Kabbalistic* concepts.

If the response is negative, either wait for another occasion or treat that lack of permission with your intention or your energy psychology of choice. Check in with yourself again, and continue as appropriate.

2. Attuning to the Letters

Look at the letters one at a time while saying their names and sounding them out. Then check yourself with

> I am aligned with God/Spirit/Higher Power
> with reference to letter... energy, or

> I am attuned with the sacred energy of the
> letter....

After testing all the letters, do adjustments for any which are weak, using your preferred method. Do a check on your correction and then test for

> I am in good alignment with the energy
> of all the letters.

You will, by now, probably test strong; if not, repeat as needed.

3. Attuning to the *Sefirot*

Consider the significance of one *Sefira* at a time, see its placement in the Tree of Life, and name it aloud. Check your energetic connection with this *Sefira*.

> I am aligned with God/Spirit/Higher Power
> with reference to *Sefira*... energy, or

> I am attuned with the sacred energy of *Sefira* ...

After testing for all the *Sefirot*, do a re-alignment where there have been any weaknesses, and then again check your results. Once you get a strong, well-aligned response with reference to each *Sefira* individually, test yourself on

> I am attuned with the energetic essences of
> all the *Sefirot*.

Again, you will probably have a strong response; if not, repeat as needed.

4. Attuning to the Concept of *Shalom*, and Bringing *Shalom* into Your Life

Check your energetic response as you look at and say the word *shalom*.

> I am attuned with all the richness of *shalom*, and allow *shalom* into my life.

Make whatever correction is needed here. Remember, it is often important to take actions in your everyday life that will help you to actualize these connections.

5 Final Step

Do a final check to address all the work you've done in an integrated way:

> I am attuned to all the Kabbalistic concepts I have worked with today.

If you still experience a weak response, or if it just feels right to do so, you can correct any remaining weakness and strengthen yourself further with an energy method, your focused intention, or an artistic creation. In addition, you can use the Temporal Tapping Technique to actively install positive attunement statements once you have corrected any misalignments.

Appendix B
Glossary

Binah - One of the *Sefirot* (see below), usually translated as Understanding.

Chesed - One of the *Sefirot*, usually translated as Mercy.

Chochmah - One of the *Sefirot*, usually translated as Wisdom.

Da'at - Sometimes considered one of the *Sefirot*, although not if *Keter* is included. Usually translated as Knowing.

Ein Sof - The name for God that suggests an infinite, eternal Being. Literally means "Without End." All forms and principles in the universe are believed to have been created from Ein Sof.

Etz Chaim - The Tree of Life, which has as one level of its meaning the usual arrangement of the *Sefirot* in a tree-like structure that can also be mapped onto the human form.

Gevurah - One of the *Sefirot*, usually translated as Judgment.

Hod - One of the *Sefirot*, usually translated as Glory.

Kabbalah - From the Hebrew root-word "to receive." The body of Jewish mysticism and esoteric thought.

Kavannah - Literally means Intention, suggests an action taken in a full-spirited way.

Keter - Generally included as one of the *Sefirot*, usually translated as Crown.

Malchut - One of the *Sefirot*, usually translated as Kingdom, refers also to Earth. Also, synonymous with *Shechinah*.

Netzach - One of the *Sefirot*, usually translated as Victory.

Ruach - The Hebrew word that means breath, wind, and spirit.

Shechinah - The feminine presence or aspect of God, dwelling on Earth.

Sefer Yetzirah - The **Book of Creation**, written between the third and sixth centuries C.E. It is the earliest metaphysical text in Hebrew.

Sefirot - The ten energy essences that are believed to underlie all that is, so that all animate and inanimate forms are said to mirror this structure. (*Sefira*- singular form).

Tiferet - One of the *Sefirot*, usually translated as Beauty.

Glossary

Tikkun olam - Literally translates as repair or correction or healing of the world. Refers to the process by which humans can act as co-creators with God so as to bring holiness to Earth.

Yesod - One of the *Sefirot,* usually translated as Foundation.

Zohar - The *Book of Splendor,* from 13th century Spain. Ascribed both to Simeon bar Yochai and to Moses de Leon. The most influential work on the Kabbalah.

Be Set Free Fast (BSFF) - An energy psychology technique. See the bibliography. Developed by Larry Nims, Ph.D.

Emotional Freedom Technique (EFT) - An energy psychology technique. See the bibliography. Developed by Gary Craig.

Tapas Acupressure Technique (TAT) - An energy psychology technique. See the bibliography. Developed by Tapas Fleming, L.Ac.

(The three above techniques are all extremely useful for releasing problems or blockages.)

Temporal Tapping Technique (TTT) - An energy approach that is helpful for "installing" positive beliefs.

Appendix C
Bibliography

Kabbalah

Berg, Rabbi Philip. (1997). *Kabbalistic astrology made easy.* New York: Research Center of Kabbalah.

Gelberman, Rabbi Joseph. (2000). *Physician of the Soul: A modern Kabbalist's approach to health and healing.* Freedom, California: The Crossing Press.

Jacobson, Rabbi Simon. (1996). *A spiritual guide to the counting of the Omer: Forty-nine steps to personal refinement according to the Jewish tradition.* Brooklyn: Vaad Hanochos Hatmimim.

Sheinkin, David. (1983). *Path of the Kabbalah.* St. Paul, Minnesota: Paragon House.

Wolf, Rabbi Laibl. (1999). *Practical Kabbalah: A guide to Jewish wisdom for everyday life.* New York: Three Rivers Press.

Energy Psychology and Muscle Testing

Craig, Gary & Fowlie, Adrienne. (1995 & 1997). *Emotional Freedom Techniques* (videotapes, audiotapes, and manual). The Sea Ranch, CA: Author.

Fleming, Tapas. (1999). *You can heal now.* Redondo Beach, CA: TAT International.

Gallo, Fred P. (1998). *Energy psychology: Explorations at the interface of energy, cognition, behavior, and health.* Boca Raton, FL: CRC Press.

Goulard, Madeline. (1999). *Inner peace: A self-help guide to emotional balance.* Ojo Caliente, NM: Simple Life Books.

Myss, Caroline. (1996). *Anatomy of the spirit.* New York: Three Rivers Press.

Nims, Larry Phillip. (1999). *Be Set Free Fast: The powerful new energy therapy...* 1431 East Chapman Avenue, Orange, CA 92866.

About the Author

Karen Kaufman Milstein has been a psychotherapist for over 30 years, with graduate degrees in both psychology and social work. She currently has a private practice in Santa Fe, New Mexico, where she lives with her husband. Dr. Milstein loves to explore both the inner spiritual world and the natural environment of New Mexico, and to weave it all together within her personal life and her practice.